TACKY

and the Emperor

HELEN LESTER

Illustrated by LYNN MUNSINGER

HOUGHTON MIFFLIN COMPANY BOSTON

Walter Lorraine Books

For Dolores Thornton — H.L.

Walter Lorraine *wᴸ* Books

Text copyright © 2000 by Helen Lester
Illustrations copyright © 2000 by Lynn Munsinger

www.houghtonmifflinbooks.com

Library of Congress Cataloging-in-Publication Data
Lester, Helen.
    Tacky and the Emperor / written by Helen Lester: illustrated by Lynn Munsinger.
        p.   cm.
    Summary: While awaiting a visit from the Emperor, a group of penguins fail to
recognize their friend Tacky in the Emperor's clothes.
        RNF ISBN 0-395-98120-4   PA ISBN 0-618-26009-9
        [1. Emperor penguin—Fiction. 2. Penguins—Fiction.] I. Munsinger, Lynn, ill. II. Title.
PZ7.L56285 Taat 2000
[E]—dc21   99-089159

Manufactured in China
SCP   10 9 8

As the sun set on the iceberg, Goodly, Lovely, Angel, Neatly,
Perfect, and Tacky were telling penguin jokes.
"Why did the penguin cross the road?" asked Goodly.
"Why?" asked his companions.
"He didn't."
Lovely, Angel, Neatly, and Perfect laughed uproariously.
They couldn't figure out what was funny, but they knew it was
polite to laugh at the end of a joke, and this seemed to be the
end of the joke.

"I don't get it," said Tacky.

"How many penguins does it take to change a light bulb?" asked Lovely.

Before anyone could answer, a messenger swooped down and dropped a note. The note read: THE EMPEROR IS COMING TO VISIT. LIKE TOMORROW.

This news put Goodly, Lovely, Angel, Neatly, and Perfect into a flap. The emperor! Their leader! They must, must, must get ready to welcome him properly.

So all through the night they twitted about.

Goodly, Lovely, and Angel made piles of fish-flavored cupcakes, mounds of fish-flavored ice cream, and gallons of fish-flavored punch.

Neatly decorated a throne with ribbons and sparkly stars.

Perfect practiced
a perfect dance for the emperor's
entertainment.

Tacky was in charge of balloons.

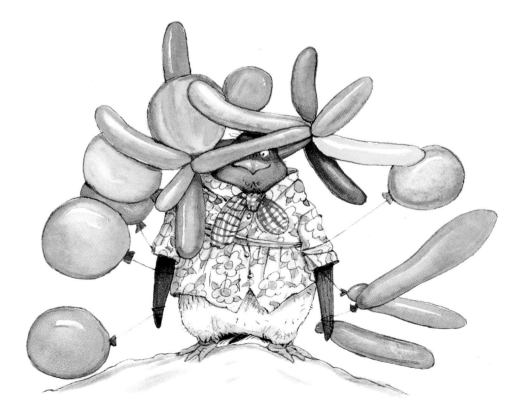

As the sun rose, he blew up the last one.
I'll make this the biggest of all, he thought.

So he huffed

and he puffed

and he rose,

and the next thing he knew,

KLINK,

he had crashed at
the foot of a very large
block of ice.
Unknown to Tacky, this
impressive block of ice
was the emperor's
palace.

The emperor had been in an especially grumpy mood, for it was hard work being an emperor.

"Visits, visits, visits," he grumbled. "What a bore. Dressing up in that uncomfortable visiting costume day in and day out. I suppose they'll have the usual fish-flavored food. And silly decorations. And dull entertainment."

And then he thought, *Perhaps a little swim will refresh me.*
So he shed his boss hat and his royal bathrobe and his curly
twinkle-toe shoes and waded into the royal swimming pool.

300 FT

"*Oooooo,* looky here!" exclaimed Tacky when he noticed the dazzling pile of clothes. "Someone has thrown out a snazzy costume!" Chuckling with excitement, he put on the boss hat and the royal bathrobe and the curly twinkle-toe shoes.

"*Ta-da!*" he chirped. "Am I ready to meet the emperor or what!"
And with that he wobbled home.

As Tacky approached Goodly, Lovely, Angel, Neatly, and Perfect in his nifty outfit, they whispered, *"Shhhh.* Here he comes! Here he comes!" And they fell to their bellies, being unable to fall to their knees because penguins don't have knees.

"Oh, Your Highness, welcome to our humble berg, welcome, welcome!"

Well, thought Tacky, *what a nice greeting.* He couldn't remember being received by his companions with such a fuss.

"Oh, Your Highness," they cried, "please honor us by sitting on
the ribbony, sparkly throne."
"Well, thanks," said Tacky. "Don't mind if I do."
He wrapped several decorative ribbons around his middle, popped
some balloons with his beak, and played Frisbee with the
sparkly stars.

His companions' beaks dropped open at this surprising behavior, but of course they said nothing. After all, *this was the emperor.* Then they encouraged him. "Please, please, Your Highness, enjoy some delicious fish-flavored refreshments."

"Don't mind if I do," said Tacky as he dived in and enjoyed everything, right down to the last slurp.

Goodly looked at Lovely, who looked at Angel, who looked at Neatly, who looked at Perfect, who looked at the empty bowls, plates, and pitchers. My, this was a hungry fellow. Rounder than they had expected, too, and certainly rounder than he'd been minutes before. Ah, but *this was the emperor*.

And according to their careful schedule, it was entertainment time. "Please, please, please, Your Highness, sit back, relax, and enjoy the perfect dance Perfect will perform for you."

"Don't mind if I do," said Tacky. Funny, Perfect had never danced for him before. Wasn't this fun.

Perfect was taking a flying leap to begin the dance when . . .

Rooty-toot-toot

Wumpa
Wumpa
Wumpa

The emperor appeared!

Oops.

The five companions looked up at the emperor.

Then across to Tacky.

Then back to the emperor.

And then they saw it. Teeny, tiny, and definitely Hawaiian, a bit of Tacky's shirt poked out of his robe.

Goodly gasped. Lovely twitched. Angel gulped.

Neatly smothered an *"eek!"* And Perfect fainted.

This was *not* the emperor, and now they realized what was happening. Or had happened.

"What's happening?" greeted Tacky, who'd been having such fun he only now remembered that the emperor was coming.

When the emperor said nothing except "Nice outfit," Tacky thought, *Hmmm. The emperor has no clothes. But this must be the Big Fella. Yup. Let's see. No decorations. Nope. No food. Nope. Showtime's over. Yup. I guess I'm on.*

Tacky quickly made a
snowball cone and offered
it to the emperor.
"Mmm," said the emperor.
"No fish."

Tacky then gathered a few
unpopped balloons
and made a lovely
decorative hat.

"Very comfortable," said the emperor.
For a grand finale, Tacky did a hoppity floppity
dance and sang his favorite song.

How many toes does a fish have?
I wonder, yup, I wonder.
And how many wings on a cow? Wow.
I wonder, yup, I wonder.

The emperor broke into a belly laugh, clapped
his flippers, and rolled on the ground.
This was the funniest entertainment he'd seen in years.

And he didn't have to admire boring decorations, eat fish-flavored food, or wear his uncomfortable visiting costume. He stayed for the whole day, sharing snowball cones and silly penguin jokes.

Why, late in the day, the emperor even tried one:

"How many penguins does it take to change a light bulb?" he asked.

"How many? How many?" begged the penguins.

"To get to the other side!" howled the emperor, and everybody had a huge laugh.

"I don't get it," said Tacky.

As the sun set, the emperor thanked the penguins for an outstanding day and told Tacky to keep the nifty costume.

"You're a prince among penguins," he said.

As the emperor waddled away, Goodly, Lovely, Angel, Neatly, and Perfect hugged "Prince" Tacky.

Tacky was an odd bird, but a nice bird to have around.